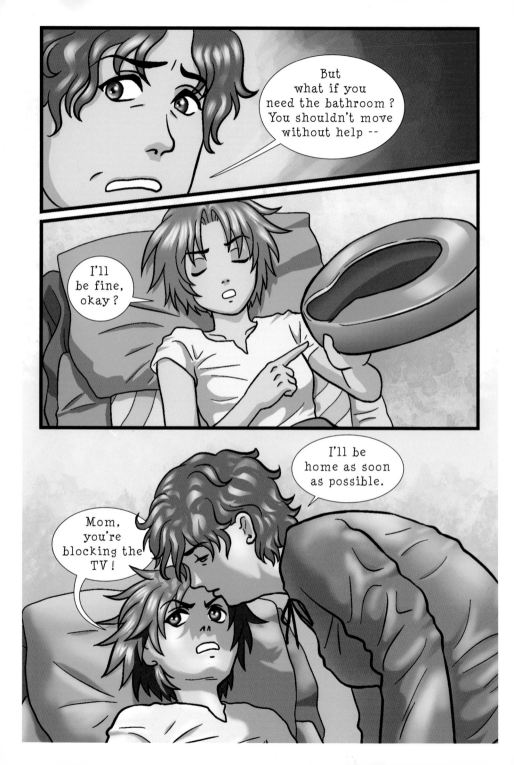

First get more light in here, then figure out what to do...

...rain...

...water...

...wet...

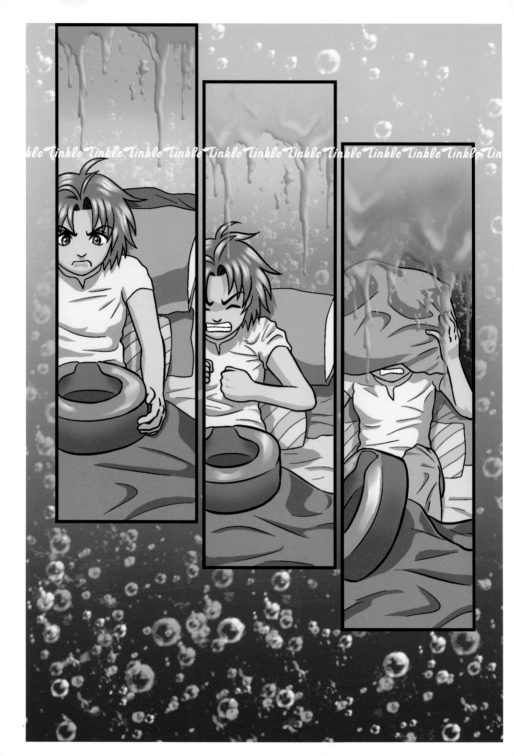

Say wha -- ? **Huh?**

Am I missing something? This doesn't make any sense!

* Serenity #2

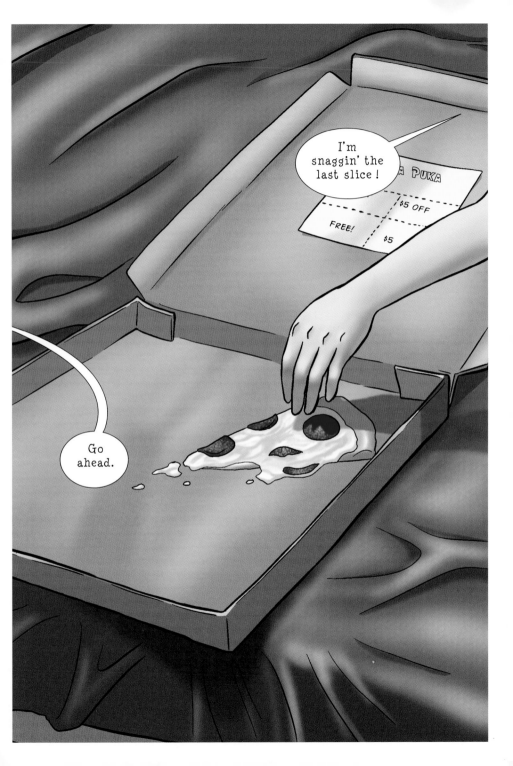

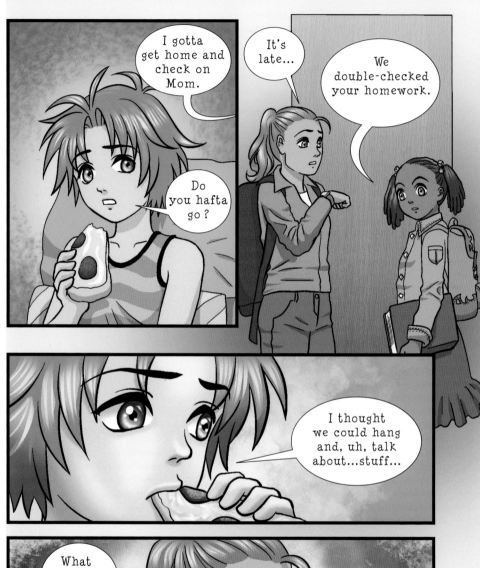

Wednesday evening, after doctor's appointment...

Okay if I go out tonight?

You broke your leg -- now you wanna **aggravate** it by **partying**!

My only aggravation -- oh, skip it! Can I go, yes or no?

Do what you want!

Just don't expect me to drive!

THE GERUNDING

Maybe it ain't worth being a Christian if I can't yell back!

Still... she didn't say I couldn't go...

Not that it would matter if she did!

But what about all those "Thou Shalt Nots..."?

Read Matthew 22:36-39.

flip-flip-flip

Try the **New** Testament...

flip-flip-flip

I know, Kimberly!

He brought a Bible to his world history class.

Ms Baxter, the ancient Jews and Christians are part of history!

The Bible is religious!

Mr. Grandy explained his lesson plan to me.

For that matter, who believes that love stuff?

=sigh=
I know I'd like to!

Here, I fixed that glitch in your mp3 player.

Solid!

There's Derek -- and no Kimberly!

El perfect-o!

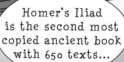

Philippians 2:11 (NCV)

"You shall love"

Life's a beach --
come and play !

"INSANELY UNIQUE !"
-- MangaPunk.com

GOOFYFOOT GURL

You can find
anything on a beach
-- especially FUN
and ROMANCE !

Making her splash in Summer 2007 !

Created by Realbuzz Studios
Published by Thomas Nelson
Find out more at
www.RealbuzzStudios.com

Wanna see ?
Turn the page for a
SPECIAL SNEAK
PREVIEW !!!

THE revolve TOUR

ALL NEW
EVENT
for Teen Girls
PRESENTED BY WOMEN OF FAITH

We're Coming to a City Near You!
TOUR DATES

Columbus, OH
September 14 - 15, 2007

Dallas, TX
September 21 - 22, 2007

Hartford, CT
September 28 - 29, 2007

St. Louis, MO
October 5 - 6, 2007

Anaheim, CA
October 12 - 13, 2007

Sacramento, CA
October 19 - 20, 2007

Philadelphia, PA
November 2 - 3, 2007

Minneapolis, MN
November 9 - 10, 2007

Portland, OR
November 16 - 17, 2007

Atlanta, GA
November 30 - Dec. 1, 2007

Orlando, FL
January 25 - 26, 2008

Charlotte, NC
February 1 - 2, 2008

Denver, CO
February 15 - 16, 2008

Houston, TX
February 22 - 23, 2008

Hawk Nelson

Natalie Grant

KJ-52

Max & Jenna Lucado

Ayiesha Woods

Chad Eastham

Kimiko Soldati

Download
Preview Video
Online

To register by phone, call 877-9-REVOLVE
or online at REVOLVETOUR.COM

Serenity

Created by Realbuzz Studios, Inc.
Min Kwon, Primary Artist

Serenity throws a big wet sloppy one out to:
Nancy D.H., Charlotte B.H., Kevin M., and Lynn F.

Smack!

Luv U Guyz !!!

©&TM 2007 by Realbuzz Studios   ISBN 978-1-59554-388-2
www.Realbuzz Studios.com
www.SerenityBuzz.com

Published by Thomas Nelson, Inc. Nashville, TN 37214 www.thomasnelson.com

Library of Congress Cataloguing-in-Publication Data
Applied For

Scripture quotations marked NCV are taken from
The HOLY BIBLE, New Century VERSION®. NCV®.
Copyright © 2001 by Nelson Bibles.
Used by permission of Thomas Nelson. All rights reserved.

Printed in Singapore.
5 4 3 2 1